Isabelle Harper

MY DOG ROSIE

Illustrated by Barry Moser

THE BLUE SKY PRESS
An Imprint of Scholastic Inc., New York

The Blue Sky Press

Text copyright © 1994 by Isabelle Harper
Illustrations copyright © 1994 by Barry Moser

For information regarding permission, please write to:
Permissions Department,
The Blue Sky Press, an imprint of Scholastic Inc.,
555 Broadway, New York, New York 10012

The Blue Sky Press is a trademark of Scholastic Inc.

Rosie, Izzy, and Barry wish to thank Alexandra Day and the folks at Farrar, Straus
& Giroux for granting permission to print the jacket of *Carl Goes Shopping*,
by Alexandra Day—Rosie's favorite book, of course! Copyright © 1989 by
Alexandra Day, used by permission of Farrar, Straus & Giroux, Inc.
Special thanks also to Friskies Pet Care, a division of Nestlé/Carnation
Food Company, for the use of their cat food in this book.
Friskies is a registered trademark of Nestlé Inc.

Library of Congress Cataloging-in-Publication Data
Harper, Isabelle.   My dog Rosie / Isabelle Harper; illustrated by Barry Moser.
p.   cm.
Summary: While her grandfather works in his studio,
a young girl takes care of the family dog.
ISBN 0-590-47619-X
1. Dogs—Fiction.   I. Moser, Barry, ill.   II. Title.
PZ7.H23133My   1994   [E]—dc20   93-45380   CIP   AC

12 11 10 9 8 7 6 5 4 3 2   4 5 6 7 8 9/9
Printed in Singapore

First printing, October 6, 1994

The illustrations in this book were executed with watercolor on paper
handmade by Simon Green at the Barcham Green Mills in Maidstone, Kent,
Great Britain, especially for the Royal Watercolor Society.
Production supervision by Angela Biola
Art direction by Kathleen Westray
Designed by Barry Moser

For Carl

WHEN GRANDPA goes into his room to work,

it's my job to take care of Rosie.

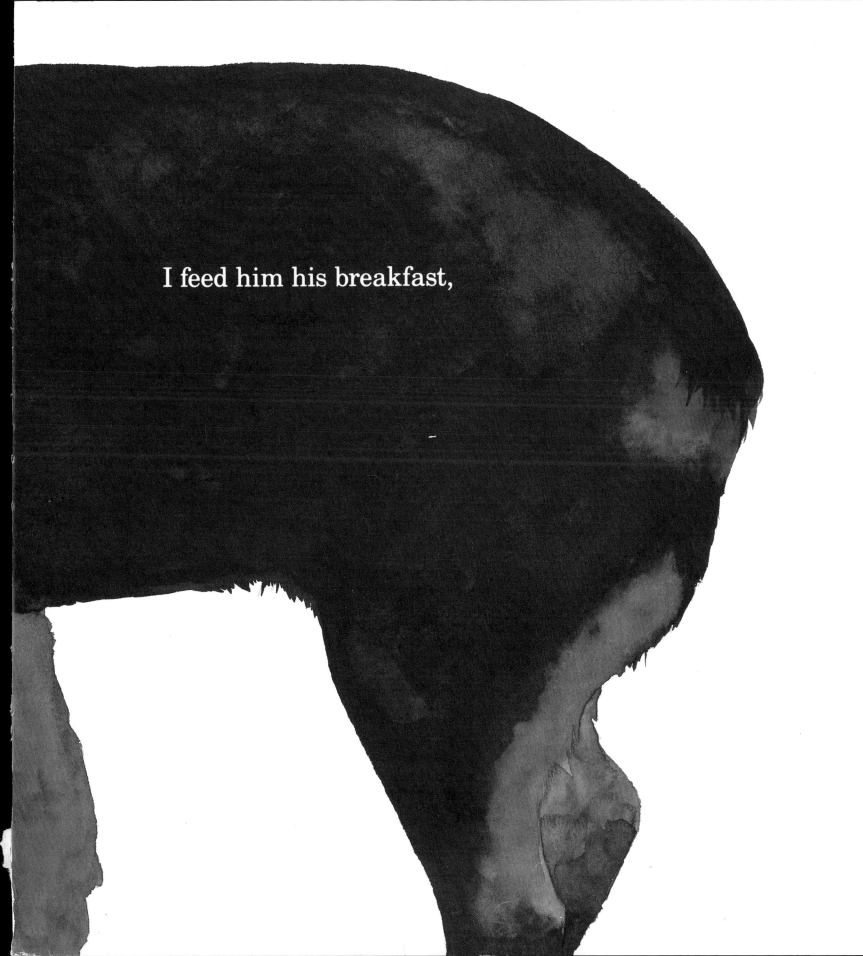

I feed him his breakfast,

I give him his bath,

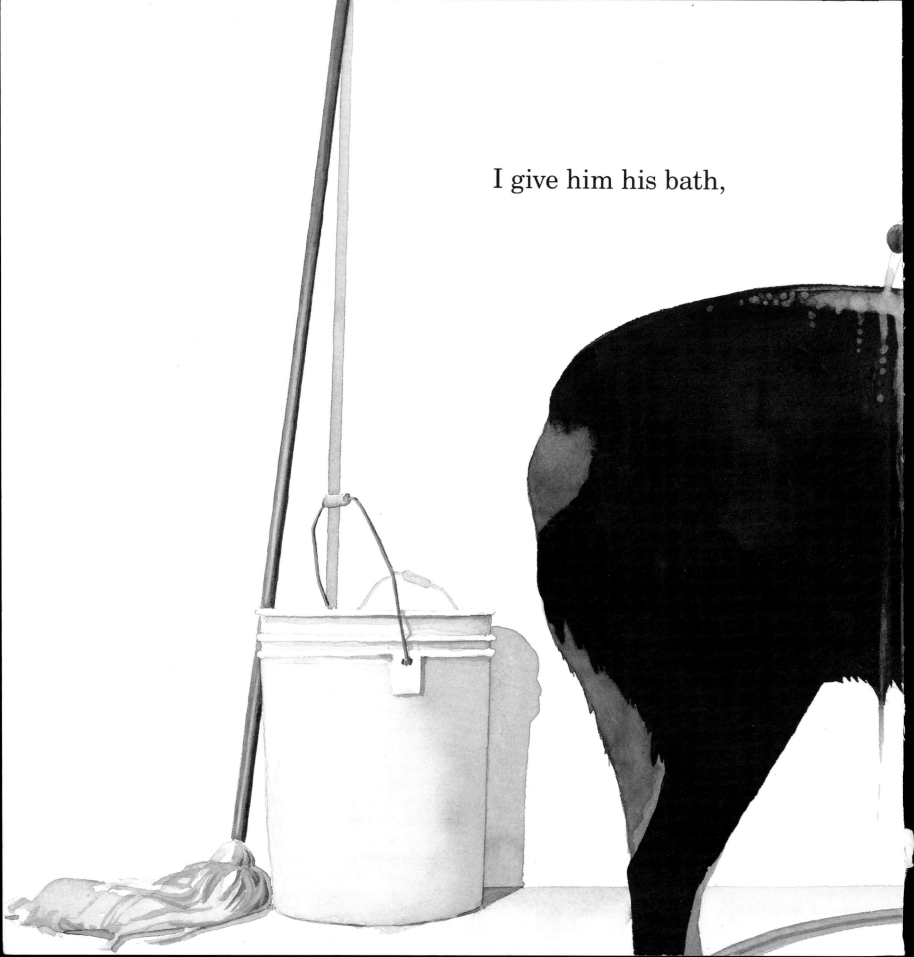

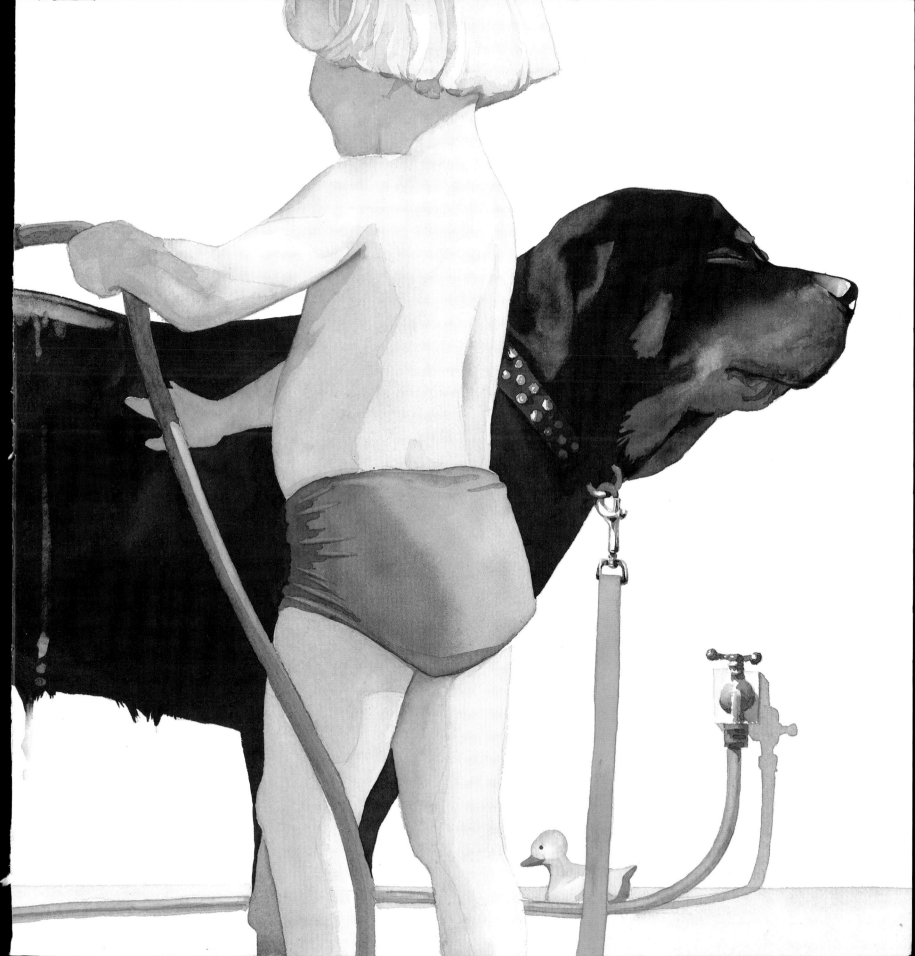

and then I help him dry off before I brush his hair.

I read him his favorite story,

and after that, I take him outside to play.

I throw the ball,

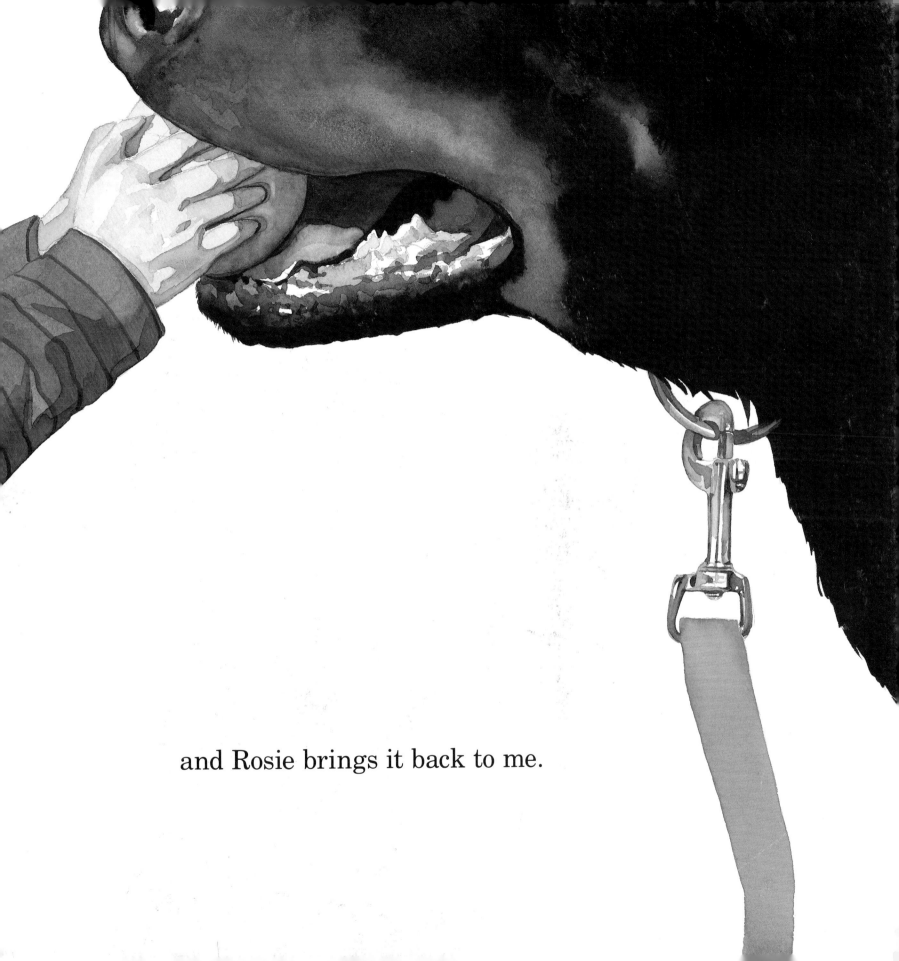

and Rosie brings it back to me.

Woodrow comes along, and he plays with us, too.

Rosie loses the ball.

Woodrow finds it and keeps it.

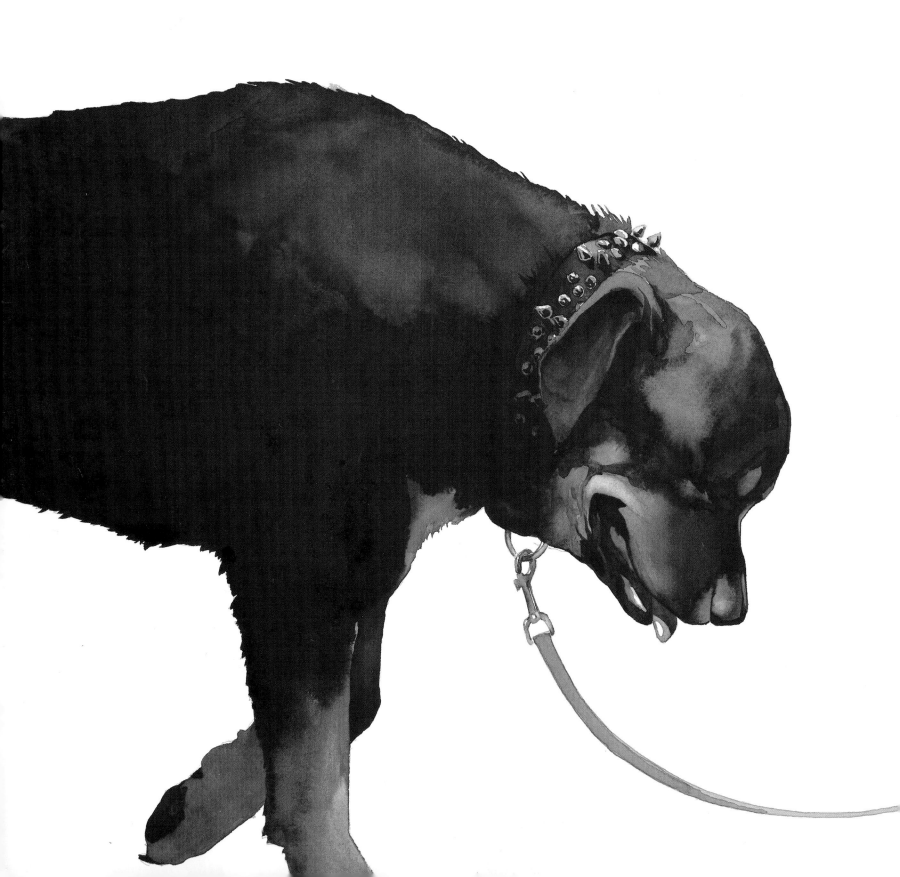

Rosie is tired. It's time for his nap.

Grandpa helps me with Rosie's quilt.

Soon Rosie is sound asleep.

"I have to go back to work now," Grandpa says.
"Will you stay here with Rosie and take care of him for me?"

"Yes."